ABOUT THE BOOK

In this cheerful portrait of seasonal change, a brother and sister take part in preparations for the coming winter. The farm bustles with activity, indoors and out, and everyone in the family shares the hard work as well as the fun. Grandma interprets ancient signs that predict extra cold months ahead, while the children, snuggling safe under their comforters, joyously wait for the first snowfall.

WINTER'S COMING

by Eve Bunting

pictures by Howard Knotts

Harcourt Brace Jovanovich
New York and London

a LET ME READ book

Library of Congress Cataloging in Publication Data

Bunting, Anne Eve.
Winter's coming.

(A Let me read book)
SUMMARY: As the seasons change, there are fatter
caterpillars, thicker corn husks, and brighter fall
leaves predicting a hard, cold winter.
[1. Winter—Fiction] I. Knotts, Howard. II. Title.
PZ7.B91527Wk [E] 76-28321
ISBN 0-15-298036-9
ISBN 0-15-298037-7 pbk.

For Christine,
who remembers only California winters

Dad says it will be a long, hard winter.
The hornets have built their paper

nests high in the eaves so that they will
be out of the deep snow.

The caterpillars are furrier this year.
Our cows are growing winter coats,

thick as blankets. Even our dog, Patch,
looks woolier. Dad says Patch knows.

Dad says it will be a long, hard winter.
He's making sure our roof has no leaks.

He's chopping wood for the woodpile.
Dad says we'll be ready too.

Grandpa says there'll be a lot of snow.
He showed us how thick the husks
have grown on his sweet corn.
The leaves this fall are all scarlet and

gold. Grandpa says he has never seen them this bright, and Grandpa has seen a lot of falls.

"See how many acorns are on the oak tree," he says.

And yesterday he found a den of eight raccoons, curled up in the corner of the barn. Grandpa says they pretty nearly scared the senses out of him.

The sky is full of ducks flying south.
The whistling swans are leaving too. By
day and by night we hear the beating of

their wings, but they leave no trace
behind them in the blue emptiness.

Grandpa says there'll be *lots* of snow.
He's making new sleds for Susie and me,

and a toboggan.
    Grandpa says then we'll be ready too.

Grandma says it will be cold this
winter. She saw four black crows on a
hickory limb.

"Four black crows mean four white snows," Grandma says.
Grandma knows.

She says there are daddy-longlegs in her kitchen. There was one in her coffee cup. They're coming inside because they know the cold's coming.

"This morning there were spider webs all over the blackthorn hedge," Grandma says. "That's a sure sign."

Grandma says it's going to be cold. She's knitting mittens and woolly scarves for Susie and me, and socks that come above our knees.

Grandma says we'll be ready.

Our house smells of apple jelly and
sweet pear syrup. The pantry shelves
are heavy with jars of purple plums and
long green pickles.

Mother is all the time filling crocks
and bottles.
"We'll be ready," she says.

Tonight, when we were in bed, she
pulled back the curtains so we could see
the sky.

"The moon's in its cradle," she said.

"It's going to be a long, hard winter."
She tucked the comforters over our toes.
    When she turned off the light, the
moon looked bigger.

"It's going to be a long, hard winter,"
Susie said. She gave a little bounce in the
bed, the way she always does when she's
pleased about something.

I snuggled down. It was warm under

the comforter.

The moon sailed through the dark
sky, like the ghost of summer.

"Good," I said.

"I hope winter comes soon."

Eve Bunting was born and educated in Ireland and came to the United States in 1959 with her husband and three children. Ms. Bunting, who now enjoys the sunshine in Pasadena, California, drew upon her memories of cold Irish winters to write this Let Me Read story. She is the author of many other children's books, and her stories have appeared in *Cricket* and *Jack and Jill*.

Howard Knotts lives in a two-hundred-year-old house in upstate New York with his wife, author and illustrator Ilse-Margret Vogel, and nine cats. Mr. Knotts, an established artist whose paintings have been widely exhibited, has written as well as illustrated several books for children.

E
Bun   Bunting, Eve
         Winter's coming

                    Copy 2

DATE DUE			

MEDIALOG
Alexandria, Ky 41001